curvy girl for the mafia daddy

emma bray

one

. . .

Luca

I'M SITTING at my mahogany desk, my fingers steepled as I gaze out at the glittering city lights below. The Rolex on my wrist ticks steadily, each second echoing in the silence of my penthouse office.

The shrill ring of my cell phone cuts through the quiet. I glance at the caller ID. It's Enzo, my most trusted advisor. He wouldn't call at this hour unless it was urgent.

I answer with a curt "What is it?" My voice is gravel.

"Boss, I have some bad news." Enzo's normally stoic tone wavers. "It's about your brother Dante..."

My grip tightens on the phone, jaw clenching. "What about him?"

There's a heavy pause. "He's dead, Boss. Shot outside his home earlier tonight. I'm so sorry."

The words hit me like a punch to the gut. I suck in a sharp breath, a storm of emotions roiling within me—shock, grief, white-hot rage.

My brother, my *blood*, gone just like that. Snuffed out by some cowardly bastard.

"Any leads on who did this?" I growl, my free hand balling into a fist.

"Not yet. But there's something else you should know..." Enzo hesitates. "Dante's wife was also killed. Their son Matteo is alive. He's only five years old."

Matteo. My nephew, now an orphan. The full weight of it hits me. This innocent boy's entire world has just shattered. And as my brother's only living relative, his care now falls to me.

I lean back in my leather chair and close my eyes for a long moment, letting the news sink in. When I open them, they blaze with renewed purpose and determination.

"Enzo, I want a status report within the hour. Mobilize every resource. We're going to find the scum who did this and make them pay." My tone is lethal calm. "And have Matteo brought to the estate immediately. He's under my protection now."

"Yes, Boss. Consider it done."

I end the call and stand, moving to the wall of windows. I press my palm to the cool glass, looking out over my dark kingdom of steel and shadow.

Everything has changed in an instant. But one thing is certain.

I will keep Matteo safe, no matter the cost. And I will rain down unholy vengeance on those who tore our family apart. This I vow, on my brother's blood.

They have no idea the hell that's coming for them.

But then I realize with a start that I don't know the first thing about caring for a child.

I pick up the phone and place a call.

———

The sharp rap of knuckles against wood jolts me from my vengeful musings. I slide my gun into its shoulder holster, schooling my features into an impenetrable mask.

"Enter."

Marco opens the door, revealing a curvaceous

young woman clutching a bag, her wide eyes taking in the opulent surroundings. Chestnut curls frame a heart-shaped face—pretty, in a girl-next-door way. Innocence radiates from her like a beacon.

Innocence has no place in my world.

"Boss, this is Dana Johnson. The nanny agency sent her."

I rake her figure with an assessing gaze, noting the way she fidgets under my scrutiny. Nervous. Good. Fear is a useful tool.

"Ms. Johnson." I inject a thread of steel into my voice. "I trust you understand the gravity of this position. Discretion is non-negotiable."

She straightens her spine, meeting my stare head-on. Unexpected. "Of course, Mr. Romano. I'm here for Matteo, nothing else."

Bold little thing. The barest hint of a smile tugs at my mouth before I banish it. "Matteo is the sole focus. You'll be at his beck and call, tending to his every need. I expect your undivided attention on him."

"I wouldn't have it any other way." Conviction rings in her tone. "Childcare is my top priority."

Admirable, but she's naively unaware of the dark undercurrents in this house. In *me*.

I close the distance between us, catching the

hitch in her breath when I invade her space. The scent of vanilla and something uniquely feminine invades my nostrils.

"One more thing." My voice is a low purr. "In this house, my word is law. Defy me..." I trail off, letting the unspoken threat hang in the air.

She tips her chin up fractionally, defiance sparking in her eyes. "I don't scare easily, Mr. Romano. And I never back down from a challenge."

Arousal courses through me, fierce and sudden. I want to snap that pretty neck. I want to bury myself inside her until she screams my name.

I do neither.

"Good." I give her a smile devoid of warmth. "Matteo's room is upstairs, third door on the left. Get to work, Ms. Johnson."

She nods, grip tightening on her bag as she walks past me.

Once she's gone, I turn to Marco, eyebrow arched. "Thoughts?"

He shrugs. "Nurturing type. Good with kids. Bit of a spitfire, though."

My eyes gleam, full of wicked promise. "It appears Ms. Johnson needs a lesson in submission."

One I'll greatly enjoy teaching her.

Three hours later, and I still can't get the damned nanny out of my head.

What the fuck is it about her?

Those luscious curves…

Those full breasts…

She's got a body on her, that's for sure. But I'm not so shallow that all I care about is looks.

It's something else.

Something I can't quite put my finger on.

I grab my laptop and pull up her file because I'm no idiot. I have a full file made of everyone who enters my domain.

No surprises that way.

Dana Johnson. 24 years old. Graduated top of her class with a degree in early childhood education. Glowing references. Not so much as a parking ticket on her record.

On paper, she's practically a saint. The perfect nanny.

But I saw the flash of defiance in her eyes. The spark of challenge when I laid down the law.

Little Ms. Johnson isn't quite the innocent angel she appears to be.

And I'm just the man to uncover her secrets.

I lean back in my chair, fingers drumming against the polished wood of my desk. I should be focusing on finding Dante's killer, on protecting Matteo, on running my empire.

Instead, I'm obsessing over a goddamn nanny.

I shake my head in disgust. *Get it together, Romano. You're not some horny teenager. You're a fucking king.*

But when I close my eyes, all I see is Dana. That sweet, curvy body. Those defiant eyes. That smart mouth that needs to be put to better use...

Fuuuuck.

I adjust myself, my cock already half-hard just thinking about her. This isn't like me. I'm always in control. Always calling the shots.

But something about her gets under my skin. Makes me want to lose control. To take her and make her *mine* in every way possible.

I need to stay away from her. For both our sakes. She's here for Matteo, not to be my plaything.

But, oh, what a curvy little plaything...

Dana

I carefully close the door to Matteo's room, relief washing over me. After a few hours of playing, reading stories, and gently soothing him, the poor little guy is finally asleep. My heart breaks for him. I can't imagine the trauma and confusion he must be feeling.

I lean against the wall for a moment, closing my eyes and just breathing. It's been a whirlwind since I arrived at the Romano estate. The sheer opulence of the place is staggering. And the man who runs it all...

Luca Romano. That name sends a shiver down my spine. He's easily the most intense, intimidating man I've ever met. Those piercing blue eyes seem to see right into my soul, stripping away every defense. And the way his suit clings to that powerful, muscular body...

No. I mentally shake myself. I can't be thinking about my boss that way. Especially not when he's just lost his brother and taken on the enormous responsibility of raising his orphaned nephew. Luca needs my help with Matteo, not my schoolgirl daydreams.

I straighten up, smoothing my skirt. I need to stay focused on what matters—taking the best possible care of that sweet, traumatized little boy. Even if his uncle does make my knees weak and my heart race.

I head downstairs in search of the kitchen, figuring I should familiarize myself with the layout of this massive house.

As I turn the corner into the lavish kitchen, I stop short. Luca is there, his back to me as he faces the marble countertop. His suit jacket is off, revealing the way his crisp white dress shirt stretches across his broad shoulders.

My breath catches in my throat. I didn't expect to run into him so soon. Or for the sight of him to affect me so viscerally.

Get a grip, Dana. He's your boss, not a GQ model.

I clear my throat softly. "Mr. Romano, I didn't mean to disturb you. I was just looking for the kitchen..."

He turns slowly, those ice blue eyes locking onto mine with laser focus. "It's Luca. Mr. Romano was my father."

"Luca," I repeat, my tongue darting out to wet my suddenly dry lips. "I just wanted to let you know that Matteo is asleep. He was understandably upset, but I managed to calm him down."

Luca nods, his gaze never leaving my face. "Good. That's...good."

Is it my imagination, or is his voice a little rougher than before? I suddenly feel too warm, too aware of him as a man, not just my employer.

"I know my way around kids pretty well," I say inanely, desperate to fill the charged silence. "I'm sure in time, with patience and love, Matteo will adjust to his new normal."

"His new normal?" Luca repeats, something dangerous flickering in his eyes. He steps closer, crowding into my space. "There's nothing normal about a five-year-old losing both parents. Nothing normal about having to live with an uncle he barely knows, in a world he has no idea about."

I stand my ground, lifting my chin. "I just meant that with the right support, Matteo can learn to cope and even thrive, despite the tragedy he's facing. He's so young. He's resilient."

Luca scoffs, a harsh sound. "Resilient? He shouldn't have to be resilient. He should have his parents. His innocence."

"You're right," I say softly. "It's not fair. None of this is fair to Matteo. But he has you now. He needs you."

Something in Luca's gaze shifts, a raw vulnerability peeking through before it's quickly shuttered. "I don't know how to do this. How to be what he needs. I'm not exactly fatherhood material."

I boldly reach out, laying my hand on his muscular forearm. His skin is warm, the dusting of hair tickling my palm. "You'll figure it out. You'll learn. And I'll be here, every step of the way. For Matteo."

His eyes drop to where my hand rests on his arm, then drags back up to my face. The air feels thick, crackling with a tension I can't name. Luca's gaze burns into me, searing me from the inside out. I know I should drop my hand, step back, put some distance between us. But I can't seem to make my body obey.

Finally, Luca clears his throat and steps back. He's all formality as he states with a nod, "Goodnight, Ms. Johnson."

He turns and leaves before I can bid him good night as well.

Leaving me there with cheeks and body burning.

Luca Romano is a dangerous man.

In more ways than one.

two

. . .

Dana

MY HEART BREAKS for this poor little boy. Orphaned at such a young age.

Does he truly understand his mommy and daddy are never coming back?

I kneel down, gently brushing a lock of chestnut hair from Matteo's forehead. "Hey there, little man. What are you drawing today?" I ask softly.

"A dinosaur," the boy murmurs, his small fingers gripping the crayon tightly. He hunches over the paper in concentration.

"That's amazing, Matteo! You're so talented." I

beam at him, admiring the colorful scribbles taking shape. "Can you tell me about your dinosaur?"

As Matteo explains each jagged line and dot, his hazel eyes bright with pride, I feel a prickling awareness creep along my spine. I glance up. Luca, Matteo's uncle, stands in the doorway, arms crossed over his broad chest as he watches us intently.

Dark and dangerous.

Unyielding.

The notorious mafia king cuts an imposing figure in his impeccable black suit, dark hair slicked back.

His chiseled jaw clenches as our eyes lock, stormy grey on emerald green.

I gulp.

A current of electricity crackles between us, raising goosebumps on my skin despite the mansion's oppressive heat. I knew exactly who Luca Romano was when the agency sent me. Ruthless. Powerful. Merciless to his enemies. But Matteo needed nurturing, and this is my calling.

I tear my gaze away, focusing again on the sweet boy beside me as he chatters on. I knew the stakes when I took this job.

But I can handle Luca. I have to—for Matteo's sake. As long as I keep my wits about me, I won't get burned by the smoldering fire always lurking behind Luca's eyes when he looks at me...

The hardened planes of his face, that full sensual mouth, the raw masculine power of him…

I force the dangerous thoughts away. Matteo. He's all that matters.

I pull the giggling boy into my lap, hugging him close as I feel Luca's presence looming behind me, his intense gaze burning into my back like a brand. The fine hairs on my nape prickle with awareness. Matteo snuggles into my embrace, his small body trusting and pliant, oblivious to the crackling tension.

"Miss Dana, look!" He holds up his drawing, a green dinosaur with a crooked smile. "He's happy now."

"He sure is, sweetheart." My voice comes out huskier than I intend. Damn Luca for rattling me without a word. "I think your dino is the happiest in the whole world, because you drew him."

Matteo beams, gap-toothed and precious. I ache to protect him, to cocoon him in love and wipe away the shadows of grief that dull his eyes when he thinks no one notices. But I feel those shadows too, lurking within me. A kinship with this orphaned boy.

I kiss the top of Matteo's head, breathing in his

sweet innocence. His tiny arms tighten around my neck trustingly. My heart swells and cracks at once. I will do anything to keep him safe. To make him feel loved and wanted. Even if that means resisting my ill-advised attraction to his devastatingly handsome uncle.

The man who could destroy me with a flick of his wrist.

I feel the weight of Luca's stare, heavy and heated, as I carefully set Matteo back onto his feet. "Why don't you go wash up for lunch, little man? I'll come get you in a few minutes."

"Okay, Miss Dana." He scampers off, clutching his precious drawing.

Slowly, I turn to face Luca. My heart pounds wildly as he devours me with his eyes, trailing over my curves with blatant hunger.

A rush of desire curls low in my belly. I clench my thighs together.

"Mr. Romano," I greet him neutrally, willing my voice not to tremble. "Is there something I can help you with?"

"You've done more than enough...Dana," He prowls closer, a panther stalking his prey. The way my name rolls off his tongue sends shivers down my spine. "Matteo seems to have taken a shine to you," he says, his deep voice resonating through my bones. He steps closer, crowding into my space until I'm enveloped by his intoxicating scent—expensive cologne, Cuban cigars, and pure, raw masculinity. "And it appears the feeling is mutual."

I tilt my chin up defiantly, meeting his penetrating gaze. "Of course. Matteo is a wonderful child. He deserves all the love and support he can get, especially after such a devastating loss."

Luca's eyes flash with an unreadable emotion. Pain? Guilt? Regret? It vanishes before I can decipher it, replaced by cool assessment as he drags his gaze over my body, setting my skin ablaze. "And you think you're the one to give it to him? To be his...nurturer?" His lips curl around the word, infusing it with dark promise.

I suppress a shiver, holding his stare boldly. "I know I am. It's what I'm here for, Mr. Romano. To care for Matteo, to guide him, to protect him."

Luca's eyes narrow. In a burst of movement, he cages me against the wall, his powerful arms braced on either side of my head. I gasp at his sudden proximity, the heat of his body seeping into mine. He leans in close, his breath ghosting across my parted lips. "You think you can protect him better than I can?" he growls, his voice a low rumble that vibrates through me. "You have no idea the dangers that surround us, little girl."

I bristle at the condescension, even as my heart races at his closeness. "I'm not a little girl, Mr. Romano. I'm a trained professional. And right now, Matteo needs more than just physical protection. He needs emotional support, stability, love. That's what I provide."

Luca's eyes flash dangerously. His hand comes up to grip my chin, tilting my face to his. "And what about what I need, Dana?" he murmurs, his gaze dropping to my lips. "What about the things I want?"

My breath hitches. "What—what do you want?" The words come out as barely a whisper.

"You know exactly what I want." His thumb drags across my lower lip, his touch searing. "I see the way you look at me when you think I'm not watching. The flush on your cheeks, the quickening of your breath. You want me too. Admit it."

"I..." My mouth runs dry. I swallow hard, my pulse pounding in my ears as Luca's thumb traces the curve of my trembling bottom lip. I can't tear my gaze away from the stormy intensity of his eyes, grey and turbulent as a tempest at sea. "I don't know what you're talking about," I breathe, but the words sound weak even to my own ears.

Luca's lips quirk in a knowing smirk. He leans in closer, until I can feel the scrape of his stubble against my cheek. "Don't play coy with me, Dana," he murmurs, his voice a dark caress. "We both know there's something between us. Something primal. Raw. Undeniable."

His hand slides from my chin to curl around the nape of my neck, his fingers tangling in my hair. I bite back a whimper as he tugs my head back, exposing the column of my throat to his heated gaze. "You can feel it too, can't you? The way your body responds to mine. The way your skin flushes and your pulse races when I'm near." His thumb traces along my pulse. "Every curve of you is mine to explore."

I try to shake my head, but his grip is unyielding. "Mr. Romano, please," I whisper, hating the breathy quaver in my voice. "This isn't appropriate. I work for you. I'm here for Matteo—"

"Shh." He silences me with a finger pressed to my lips.

And then just as suddenly as he descended upon me, he steps back.

He doesn't speak another word to me. Just turns and walks away, leaving me to wonder if I imagined the whole thing.

three

. . .

Luca

I STORM out of the room, my heart pounding and my blood rushing. Damn it, I almost lost control in there. The temptation to push Dana up against the wall, hike up that tight skirt over her luscious curves and claim her right then and there was overwhelming.

"Get it together," I growl under my breath as I stalk down the hallway. But images of her voluptuous body pressed against mine, those full lips parted in surprise and desire, flash through my mind. The ache in my groin is excruciating.

Slamming open the door to my room, I head

straight for the bathroom. I barely get my zipper down before my rock-hard cock springs free. Wrapping my hand around my throbbing shaft, I grunt as I start to stroke furiously.

All I can think about is Dana—her creamy skin, the swell of her breasts straining against that prim buttoned blouse, the fire in her emerald eyes when she stands up to me. I imagine bending her over, hearing her moan as I fill her completely.

"Fuck," I groan, pumping harder and faster. The pleasure coils tighter and tighter until it explodes in a blinding rush. I bite back a roar as I come hard, spilling into my hand.

Chest heaving, I brace myself against the sink. But the release does nothing to quench the dark hunger Dana has ignited inside me. I want her—all of her.

And I won't stop until that sexy, stubborn woman is *mine*.

———

Over the next few days, I watch Dana like a hawk, my desire growing with every passing moment. She's so natural with Matteo, her gentle laugh ringing through the house as she plays with him. The way her eyes sparkle with warmth and affection for my nephew twists something deep inside me.

But it's the glimpses of her lush curves as she moves, the elegant line of her neck, the subtle sway of her hips that keep me in a constant state of painful arousal.

I find myself engineering excuses to check on her. Each fleeting glimpse is a sweet torment. I have to bite my cheek to keep from pulling her into my arms, from taking that rosebud mouth in a brutal, claiming kiss.

It's maddening, this relentless need. My balls ache and my cock throbs, straining against my zipper every time she's near. I'm like a horny fucking teenager, running off to jack off three, four times a day. Her scent, her voice, the way she looks at me from under those long lashes—it all winds me tighter and tighter until I'm ready to snap.

In the dark solitude of my bedroom, I wrap my hand around my rigid length, imagining it's her silky fingers stroking me. I picture throwing her down on my bed, ripping off those prim skirts and cardigans to reveal the tempting curves hidden underneath. I'd worship every inch of her soft skin until she's writhing and begging, then bury myself to the hilt in her wet heat. The image of her lush tits bouncing as I pound into her is enough to send me over the edge embarrassingly fast every single time.

But it's not enough. It's never enough. This insatiable hunger is clawing at my insides, demanding I make Dana mine in every way. I want to taste her, touch her, claim her so completely that she forgets any other man exists. I want to make her scream my name as I give her pleasure she's never known before.

I don't just want her body. I want everything—her mind, her heart, her very soul. And I won't rest until all of her belongs to me.

The urge to simply take what I desire is a living, breathing thing inside me. It prowls through my veins, growing more feral and harder to control by the second. My infamous restraint is eroding, my darkest instincts howling to be let loose.

I know it's wrong. I know I should keep my distance. But with every smile, every laugh, every goddamn maddening sway of her hips, Dana is breaking down my defenses. She has no idea that she's playing with fire, dancing closer and closer to an inferno that will consume us both.

I don't know how much longer I can hold back the beast clawing to break free. But there's one thing I do know as I watch her, my heart pounding and my body coiled with barely leashed need.

Come hell or high water, I *will* make Dana mine.

I scowl as I realize I've been sitting at my desk for an hour thinking about *her*. Madonn', what this woman is doing to me. I should be focused on revenge—not on how to get into the nanny's panties.

I bark out a curse and rise abruptly from my chair, stalking over to the window. The sprawling grounds of the estate stretch out before me but I don't see them. All I can see is Dana—laughing with Matteo, sunlight catching the hints of gold in her chestnut hair, her ripe curves swaying as she walks.

She's under my skin, burrowing deeper with every passing second. I feel like a junkie, craving my next hit. Except my drug of choice is five-foot-four, with piercing green eyes and an ass that makes my cock salivate.

I lean my forehead against the cool glass, trying to regain some semblance of control. But it's no use. My mind keeps conjuring up the sound of her husky laugh, the fullness of her lips, the way her hips sway as she walks away from me. I'm hard as a fucking rock just thinking about her.

I fist my hands on the windowseal.

I need to get a grip. I'm Luca Romano, for Christ's sake. I run the most powerful mafia family on the East Coast. Men tremble when I walk into a room. I take what I want, when I want it.

But with Dana, it's different. For the first time, I find myself hesitating, questioning my next move. I want her so badly it's like a physical ache, but something holds me back.

Maybe it's the way she looks at Matteo, with such tenderness and care. The way she's thrown herself into this new role, determined to give him the love and stability he needs. It stirs something foreign in my chest, something dangerously close to admiration. Respect.

I shake my head with a growl of frustration.

I can't afford to go soft, not now, not ever. Not in this world I've chosen, where any weakness is a liability that can get you killed. I've fought too hard, sacrificed too much to let a pair of green eyes and a sweet ass throw me off my game.

But damn if Dana doesn't make me want to throw out every rule I've ever made for myself. The need to possess her, body and soul, is like a fever in my blood. I want to lock her away from the world and keep her all for myself.

I curse under my breath and stalk out of my office, determined to put the curvy fucking nanny out of my mind.

four

. . .

Dana

I PAUSE outside Luca's study, which is cracked open. I haven't spoken to him since our last charged interaction, though I still can't get it out of my mind.

That domineering glint in his piercing blue eyes as he pulled me close, his powerful body pressing against my curves...*No.* I shake my head. The further I stay away from the notorious mafia king, the better.

But then I hear it. A choked sob, barely audible through the cracked door. Against my better judgment, I inch closer, peering inside.

Luca sits at his mahogany desk, head in his hands, broad shoulders shaking. Anguished gasps rack his muscular frame. In this unguarded moment, the ferocious mafia leader looks utterly...broken.

My chest constricts. I've never seen Luca like this—so raw, so human. The urge to go to him, to offer solace, builds inside me.

But I know better than to cross that threshold, so I don't.

I inch away and head to my room, but my perception of him is forever changed.

———

Luca

A single tear rolls down my cheek and splashes onto the framed photo of my brother Marco clutched in my trembling hands. My eyes burn but I blink back more tears, clenching my jaw.

I shouldn't let my guard down, even for a moment. If someone saw me, the notorious Luca Romano, reduced to a blubbering mess.

Pathetic.

Weak.

But the grief caught me off guard. It slammed into me like a punch to the gut, and now here I am doing something I *never* do.

I'm sitting her crying like a fucking woman. I disgust myself.

I sniff and wipe my eyes, scowling as I get myself under control.

I slam the photo face down on the desk and push to my feet, pacing to the window. Crossing my arms, I stare out at the sprawling estate grounds, not really seeing them.

All I can see is Dante's face. My brother. My responsibility. And I failed him.

Self-loathing sears through me and I welcome the familiar burn of it. It's better than the alternative—that aching chasm of loss that threatens to swallow me whole.

A soft knock at the door startles me and I whirl around, my hand instinctively going to the gun holstered at my side.

I narrow my eyes at the door, barking out a gruff "What?"

The door opens and Marco steps in, his expression carefully neutral. "Sorry to interrupt, Sir. But I thought you should know—Dana took Matteo off the premises. For ice cream, apparently."

Red hot fury explodes through my veins, searing away any traces of weakness. How dare she? I trusted her with my nephew, and this is what she does?

I slam my fist on the desk, relishing the sharp sting of pain. It clears my head, focuses me.

"Where?" I growl, already moving toward the door.

Marco steps back, giving me a wide berth. Smart man. "The gelato shop in town, I believe."

I don't waste time with more questions. I'm already out the door, stalking down the hallway with a singular purpose: to find them and bring them back. Now.

How could she be so reckless, so stupid?

———

Dana

I sit across from Matteo in a cozy corner booth at the bustling gelato shop, his little legs swinging under the table as he eagerly licks his double scoop of stracciatella. A smile curves my lips, seeing the pure joy radiating from him. The poor boy has been through so much lately. I thought some sugar and sprinkles could bring a little light back into those big brown eyes.

The door chimes and a hush falls over the previously lively shop. My heart drops into my stomach as I look up and see *him*.

Luca.

And he looks furious.

He stands in the doorway, his imposing frame filling it, his expression thunderous. Those piercing blue eyes blaze with barely contained fury as they lock onto me. He looks like the very devil himself, darkness swirling around him, ready to drag me under.

Matteo oblivous to the storm approaching waves his spoon in the air happily. "Zio Luca," he chirps happily. "Look, I've got gelato."

Luca doesn't even spare the boy a glance. He starts toward us, his stride predatory, his eyes never leaving mine. The other patrons scurry out of his way, pressing themselves against the cheery striped walls.

I swallow hard but lift my chin. I won't let him intimidate me.

He stops at our booth, towering over us, his hands clenched at his sides. "What the hell do you think you're doing?" he growls, his deep voice vibrating through me.

"I'm taking Matteo for gelato," I reply evenly, trying to keep the tremor from my voice. "He deserves to feel like a normal kid sometimes."

Luca slams his palms on the table, making Matteo and I both jump. He leans in close, his face a mere inch from mine. The spicy scent of his cologne invades my senses.

"You had no right," he snarls. "No right to take him off the premises without my permission. It's too dangerous."

Anger flares in my chest and I meet his seething gaze head on. "He's a child, Mr. Romano. He needs more than just rules and guards. He needs moments like this." I gesture at the half-eaten gelato.

Luca scoffs harshly. "What he needs is to stay alive. And I can't ensure that if you're going to pull stunts like this."

His words are like a slap and I flinch. Matteo's chin begins to wobble, tears welling in his eyes.

Luca notices and some of the fury bleeds from his expression. He straightens, running a hand over his face.

"Come on. We're leaving," he says, his tone brokering no argument.

Matteo's bottom lip trembles but he obediently slides out of the booth. I clench my jaw but obey.

There's nothing but silence as Luca walks us outside. He hands Matteo off to his head of security. "Take him directly home," he instructs him.

I move to follow Matteo, but Luca's hand grabs my arm like a band of iron. "You're coming with me," he growls. He opens the backdoor of his town car and pushes me into the backseat, barking at his driver to drive.

The air crackles with tension as Luca settles into the backseat beside me, slamming the door with a resounding thud. His overwhelming presence fills the confined space, his fury a palpable force pressing against my skin.

I press myself against the cool leather, putting as much distance between us as possible in the small backseat. But there's no escaping the heat of his furious gaze. It scorches me, sending a shiver down my spine that's equal parts fear and...something else. Something I refuse to acknowledge.

"What the hell were you thinking?" Luca snarls, his deep voice reverberating through the car. "Taking Matteo out in public like that, without any security? Without telling me?"

I lift my chin defiantly, even as my heart races in my chest. "He's a little boy. He deserves to have normal childhood experiences. You can't keep him locked away forever."

Luca leans in closer, his face a mere breath from mine. The spicy scent of his cologne invades my senses, making my head spin. "You have no idea the dangers that are out there. The threats against my family. I'm trying to keep him safe. And you're undermining that with your recklessness."

Anger flares hot in my veins and I glare right back at him. "Recklessness? I'm thinking about his emotional well-being. Something you clearly know nothing about, you cold, heartless bastard."

Luca's eyes flash dangerously and before I can blink, he has me pinned against the leather seat, his hard body pressing into my soft curves. I gasp at the sudden contact, heat unfurling deep in my belly.

Luca's hand slides up my thigh, his touch searing through the thin fabric of my skirt. His eyes blaze with a dangerous mix of anger and desire as they bore into mine.

"Cold and heartless?" he growls, his breath hot against my ear. "You have no fucking idea what I feel. The lengths I would go to protect what's mine."

His possessive grip tightens on my thigh and a traitorous shiver runs through me. I should push him away. I should be disgusted by his brutish behavior.

But my body betrays me, arching into his touch, craving more. Craving *him*.

"I'm not yours," I manage to get out, but my breathless voice lacks conviction.

A dark chuckle rumbles from Luca's chest. "No?" His hand slides higher, grazing the lace edge of my panties. I barely suppress a moan. "Your body tells a different story, dolcezza."

His fingers brush against my covered sex and a whimper escapes me. He groans, pressing his hardness against my hip. "Fuck, you're already wet for me."

Shame and desire war within me as he strokes me through the damp lace. I should stop this. It's wrong. He's dangerous.

But it feels so right.

I'm saved from my internal battle as the car glides to a stop.

Luca pulls back slightly, his heated gaze locking with mine. "This isn't over," he promises darkly. Then he's gone, the car door slamming behind him.

I sit there for a moment, my chest heaving, my body thrumming with unsatisfied desire. What the hell just happened?

five

. . .

Luca

I SLAM the phone down on my mahogany desk, the plastic cracking from the impact. A cold rage seizes my body as the words of the rival Ricci family's threat echo in my mind.

They dare to threaten my family, my territory. Matteo, innocent in his youth.

First this mess with Dana taking Matteo from the premises and now this.

And Dana...bellissima Dana with her soft curves and defiant eyes. Fear claws at my chest as I imagine them knowing about her.

I clench my fists, picturing their faces. No one will lay a finger on what's *mine*.

I storm out of my office, barking orders at my men. "Double the security detail. No one gets in or out without thorough checks. And find out how the hell the Riccis got this number!"

My pulse pounds as I stride down the hallway towards the nursery where Dana watches over Matteo. I need to see them, confirm they're unharmed with my own eyes. Shoving open the door, relief crashes over me at the sight of Dana in the floor playing with Matteo. Her green eyes widen as she takes in my thunderous expression.

She looks up at me warily and no wonder. Hell, twice now I've basically assaulted her and almost fucked her.

I run a hand over my face. "We need to talk. Put Matteo down for his nap, and then come to my office"

Dana rises slowly from the floor, her eyes never leaving mine. She doesn't say a word as she moves to do as she's told.

Less than twenty minutes later, she's in my study.

"What's going on?" Her voice is steady but I can see the apprehension in the set of her shoulders.

I take a deep breath, trying to rein in my raging emotions. "There's been a threat."

Her hand flies to her mouth, eyes wide with fear. "Oh my God..." She glances at my nephew, happily playing with his blocks, oblivious to the danger that swirls around us.

"I'm handling it," I grit out. "No one will touch him. Or you." The words are a vow, a promise I intend to keep at all costs.

She steps closer, her scent of vanilla and something uniquely Dana invading my senses. "Mr. Romano, I..." Her hand reaches out as if to touch me, but she lets it drop.

The air between us crackles with tension, that ever-present pull that draws me to her like a moth to a flame.

But I can't allow it. Can't let her get close only to become a target.

I take a step back, hardening my expression. "I think it's best if you leave, Dana. At least until this situation is under control."

Hurt flashes across her face before indignation takes over. "Leave? I'm not going anywhere! Matteo needs me. I need..." She cuts herself off, biting her lip.

"You need what, Dana?" I demand, my voice

rough with the desire I'm barely keeping in check. "What is it you need?"

She meets my gaze head-on, a flicker of defiance in her green eyes. "I need to feel safe. And believe it or not, I feel safe with you."

Her words knock the breath from my lungs. Christ, she has no idea what she does to me. How badly I want to haul her against me and claim her pretty mouth, consequences be damned.

But the consequences could be her life. And that is not a risk I'm willing to take.

I shake my head, a mirthless chuckle escaping me. "You shouldn't feel safe with me, bella. My world...it's no place for someone like you. All I'll bring you is pain and danger."

She takes a step closer, the heat of her body searing me even from a distance. "I'm not as fragile as you think. And I'm already in your world, whether you like it or not."

I curse under my breath, dragging a hand through my hair. She's right and I hate it. Hate that my life has touched hers, tainted her with its darkness.

"I can protect you better from a distance," I rasp, but even I can hear the lack of conviction in my voice.

Dana closes the remaining space between us to

stand directly in front of me. She looks up at me beautifully defiant. "I don't want your protection from a distance." Her voice is low, breathy. It wraps around me like a caress, weakening my resolve.

"Dana..." It's a warning and a plea.

Her fingers curl into the lapels of my suit jacket, her grip surprisingly strong for such delicate hands. "I'm not going anywhere, Luca."

The sound of my name on her lips, so soft and yet filled with steel, is my undoing.

With a muttered oath, I wrap my arms around her waist and haul her against my chest. Her soft gasp mingles with my groan as our bodies collide. Every lush curve molds against the hard planes of my muscles.

"You don't know what you're asking for," I growl, my lips a hair's breadth from hers. "If you stay, I won't be able to keep my hands off you."

She gasps, her lips parting in surprise, and I seize the opportunity to crash my mouth against hers in a bruising kiss. The first brush of her soft lips against mine ignites a fire in my blood. I groan into her mouth as I deepen the kiss, my tongue plundering the sweet cavern of her mouth.

Dana whimpers and melts against me, her fingers tightening their grip on my lapels. I walk us backwards until her luscious backside hits my desk. With a swipe of my arm, I send the contents of the desk clattering to the floor. Then I'm lifting her by the hips and setting her on the edge, never breaking the hungry seal of our lips.

I wedge myself between her parted thighs, the heat of her core scorching me even through the layers of our clothing. My hands skim down her sides to grip her lush hips, fingers digging into the giving flesh. Dana throws her head back on a gasp as I trail open-mouthed kisses along the column of her throat, my teeth scraping against her jumping pulse.

"Luca," she pants, my name a plea and prayer on her kiss-swollen lips. The sound shoots straight to my aching cock.

I reclaim her mouth in a deep, drugging kiss as I grind myself against the apex of her thighs. She's so warm, so soft, so fucking *perfect*. And she's mine. All *mine*. The thought roars through me, primal and possessive.

Dana meets each roll of my hips with her own, her legs coming up to wrap around my waist and pull me closer. And fuck, the knowledge that this curvy goddess wants me back is almost enough to make me nut right here and now.

I can feel the damp heat of her through my slacks, and it makes me wild. I thrust against her harder, faster, chasing the release that coils tighter and tighter at the base of my spine.

"That's it, baby," I encourage her, my voice rough with lust. "Let go for me. I've got you."

She keens, a high, desperate sound, and then she's shattering in my arms. Her body goes taut and then trembles as her orgasm crashes over her. The sight of her, the feel of her clenching around me, even with clothes between us, catapults me over the edge.

I bury my face in the crook of her neck to muffle my shout as I come, my hips juddering against hers. Dana holds me through it, her fingers gentle in my hair, her lips at my temple.

As the aftershocks subside, I lift my head to look at her. Her eyes are heavy-lidded, her cheeks flushed a beautiful pink. I know I should pull away, put distance between us. But I can't seem to make myself let her go.

"Dana." Her name is gravel in my throat. "Tell me to stop. Because if you don't, I'm going to strip you bare, lay you out on this desk, and make you mine in every sense of the word."

Dana moistens her lips, her chest heaving with each rapid breath. "No," she whispers. "I won't tell you to stop."

Those breathy words are my undoing. A growl

rumbles from my chest as I capture her mouth in a searing kiss, pouring every ounce of my desire into the melding of our lips.

My hands make quick work of the buttons on her blouse, desperation making my movements clumsy. I need to feel her skin against mine like I need air in my lungs.

Dana's hands are just as eager, tugging at my belt, my zipper. The sound of fabric tearing barely registers as I shrug out of my shirt, sending buttons flying. Her nails rake down my chest, leaving trails of fire in their wake.

"Fuck, Dana," I groan as I cup her breasts, the heavy weight of them perfect in my palms. Her nipples strain against the lacy confines of her bra, begging for my touch. I oblige, pinching and rolling the hardened peaks until she's writhing beneath me.

I've never wanted a woman the way I want her. It's a hunger that consumes me, a need that pounds through my veins with every frantic beat of my heart.

The lace of her bra gives way under my impatient hands. And then I'm feasting on the rosy peaks, drawing one into my mouth to suckle and nip. Dana arches off the desk, a throaty moan spilling from her lips. The sound only spurs me on, makes me suck harder.

I switch to the other breast, lavishing it with the same attention. I could spend hours worshipping her tits, but the throbbing ache in my cock demands more. Demands all of her.

My hand slides under her skirt, fingers brushing against the damp lace of her panties. She's fucking soaked, the evidence of her arousal coating my fingers as I nudge the flimsy fabric aside.

"Christ, you're dripping," I rasp, my voice guttural with lust. "Is this all for me, sweetheart?"

Dana nods frantically, her hips canting up in search of my touch. "Yes, Luca. Only for you."

Satisfaction and possessiveness surge through me at her breathy declaration. My fingers delve through her slick folds to find her clit. I circle the swollen nub, reveling in the way her body jumps and quivers under my touch.

"Please," she whimpers, nails biting into the flesh of my shoulders. "I need..."

"What do you need, Dana?" I demand, my fingers teasing her entrance. "Tell me."

Her head thrashes against the desk, her hips bucking restlessly. "You. I need you inside me. Please, Luca."

My control snaps at her plea. In an instant, I've shoved her skirt up around her waist and torn her panties off. The sight of her laid out before me, flushed and wanting, nearly brings me to my knees.

I free my straining erection from the confines of my slacks and position myself at her entrance, the broad head of my cock nudging against her slick folds.

Dana's breath hitches, her eyes wide and dark with desire as she looks up at me. I pause, searching her face for any sign of hesitation or doubt.

"Are you sure, baby?" I ask, my voice rough with restraint. "Once I'm inside you, there's no going back. You'll be mine completely."

Her hands come up to frame my face, her touch gentle despite the urgency thrumming between us. "I'm sure, Luca. I want this. I want you."

With a groan, I surge forward, burying myself to the hilt in her tight, wet heat. But instead of the smooth glide I'm expecting, I'm met with resistance. Dana cries out, her fingers digging into my biceps as her face contorts in pain.

Shock crashes over me as realization dawns. She's a virgin. Untouched. And I've just torn through her innocence with my selfish lust.

"Fuck, Dana," I rasp, stilling my hips with

immense effort. "You're...I didn't know...I'm so sorry, baby."

Tears leak from the corners of her eyes, but she shakes her head. "Don't be sorry. I wanted it to be you. Only you." She rolls her hips tentatively, taking me even deeper.

Possessiveness roars through my veins at her words, at the knowledge that no other man has ever touched her like this. That I'm the first and only one to lay claim to her sweet body.

"Mine," I growl, pulling out slowly before thrusting back in. "You're mine now, Dana. Your perfect little cunt belongs to me. No other man will ever have you like this."

She gasps and arches into me, her channel fluttering around my invading cock. "Yes, Luca. I'm yours. Only yours."

I set a hard, driving pace, my hips slapping against the backs of her thighs with each forceful thrust. The desk creaks beneath us, the sound mingling with our harsh pants and moans.

"That's it, baby," I encourage her as I feel her start to tighten around me. "Squeeze my cock with this tight little pussy. Milk me dry."

Dana throws her head back with a keening cry, her nails raking angry red lines down my back as she comes apart. Her cunt clamps down on me like a vice, the rippling walls pushing me closer to the edge.

I grit my teeth, determined to wring every last ounce of pleasure from her quivering body. Shifting the angle of my hips, I grind against her swollen clit with each pass, prolonging her climax.

"Oh God, Luca!" She sobs, trembling violently as a second orgasm crashes over her on the heels of the first. The sensation is too much, too intense.

With a roar, I bury myself to the hilt inside her one last time and let go, spilling myself deep in her clenching heat.

I collapse on top of her, my face buried in the crook of her neck as aftershocks course through my spent body. Dana's arms come around me, holding me close as our racing hearts gradually slow.

In the aftermath of our passion, the reality of what I've done comes crashing down on me. I've taken her virginity, claimed her in the most primal way possible. And in doing so, I've irrevocably tied her to me and my dark, dangerous world.

Self-loathing rises like bile in my throat. She deserves better than this, better than me. I'm a monster, a killer. My hands are stained with blood that will never wash clean. How can I taint her purity with my filth?

Slowly, I raise myself up on my elbows to look

down at her. Her eyes are closed, her lips parted and swollen from my kisses. She looks thoroughly debauched, and so fucking beautiful it makes my chest ache.

"Dana," I rasp, my voice hoarse with emotion. "Open your eyes, sweetheart."

Her lashes flutter and then lift, revealing those stunning green depths. They widen slightly as she takes in my serious expression.

"I'm so sorry," I tell her, the words inadequate but all I have. "I shouldn't have...fuck, I took advantage of you. You were a virgin and I—"

She presses her fingers to my lips, silencing my self-recrimination. "No, Luca. You didn't take advantage. I wanted this, wanted you. I still do."

I shake my head, marveling at her capacity for forgiveness. "You don't know what you're saying. Being with me...it's not safe. The threats, the danger that surrounds me, it will consume you too."

Determination hardens her delicate features. "I'm not afraid. Whatever comes, we'll face it together. I'm not going anywhere, Luca. I'm yours now, remember?"

My heart clenches at her words, at the unwavering loyalty shining in her eyes. I don't deserve it, don't deserve her. But God help me, I'm too selfish to let her go.

"Mine," I agree roughly, lowering my head to claim her lips in a searing kiss, pouring all my fear and love and desperate need into the press of my mouth on hers.

She meets me with equal fervor, her tongue tangling with mine as she arches up into my body. And just like that, the embers of my desire flare back to life. I groan into her mouth as I feel myself hardening inside her once more.

Dana gasps as I begin to move, my hips rocking in a slow, deep rhythm. "Luca," she breathes, her hands gliding over the taut muscles of my back. "You feel so good."

A guttural groan tears from my throat at her breathy words. I pull back, nearly withdrawing completely before surging forward again, burying myself to the hilt in her tight, slick heat.

"Cazzo, you're still so tight," I rasp against the shell of her ear. "Your sweet little cunt fits me like a glove."

Dana mewls, her inner muscles fluttering around my pistoning cock. I set a deep, rolling pace, pulling out slowly only to slam back in, over and over until she's writhing beneath me.

"That's it, tesoro," I encourage her, angling my hips to hit that spot deep inside her that makes her eyes roll back. "Take what you need. Use me for your pleasure."

She does just that, her hips rising to meet my every thrust, her blunt nails digging into my shoulders. I relish the sting, the physical proof of her desire, her need for me.

I bend my head, capturing one rosy nipple between my lips. I lave the sensitive bud with my tongue before grazing it with my teeth. Dana jolts as if electrified, a high keen escaping her kiss-swollen lips.

"Luca, please," she pants, her head thrashing against the desk. "I'm so close..."

I double my efforts, suckling her nipple harder as I reach between our sweat-slicked bodies to circle her clit with my thumb.

"Come for me, amore," I command, my voice rough with strain. "Soak my cock with your sweet cream."

As if on cue, her body goes rigid, bowing up off the desk as her climax crashes over her. I muffle her scream with my mouth, swallowing down her cries of ecstasy even as my own orgasm surges through me.

I empty myself deep inside her, painting her womb with jet after jet of my seed. Merda, what if I've gotten her pregnant? My pleasure only intensifies at the thought of her belly swelling with my child.

But then I picture it—Dana, glowing and round with new life, a life we created together.

The image steals my breath even as it terrifies me.

I collapse on top of her, my face buried in the crook of her neck as we both struggle to catch our breath. Her fingers card gently through my sweat-dampened hair, soothing me.

"Ti amo, Luca," she whispers, so softly I almost think I've imagined it.

My heart stutters in my chest. She loves me. This incredible, brave, beautiful woman loves me. Me, a hardened mafioso with blood on his hands. I don't deserve her love, but I'm too much of a selfish bastard to refuse it.

I lift my head from the crook of her neck to gaze down at her. Her green eyes shine with tenderness and sincerity, stealing the air from my lungs.

"Dana," I rasp, my voice rough with emotion. "You can't...you shouldn't love me. I'm no good for you, tesoro."

She shakes her head, a sad smile curving her kiss-swollen lips. "It's too late, Luca. My heart is already yours, flaws and all. And I'm not letting you go."

My chest tightens, fear and wonder warring within me. I've never needed anyone the way I need her. Never wanted to claim someone so completely, body and soul.

"I love you too, bella," I confess as I tighten my arms around her soft curves possessively.

And I vow here and now that I will do whatever it takes to keep her safe.

six

. . .

Dana

I FREEZE as the office door slams open, nearly hitting the wall. Luca storms out, his face a mask of fury. His piercing blue eyes lock onto mine, and I feel a shiver run down my spine.

"We need to talk," he growls, stalking towards me. "Now."

My heart races as I follow him into his private study, the click of the lock echoing like a gunshot. He paces the room like a caged panther, his muscles coiled with tension.

"There's a traitor in our midst," Luca snarls,

slamming his fist on the mahogany desk. "Someone I trusted, working for those bastards."

Fear grips me, both for him and for us. Matteo most of all. I step closer, wanting to comfort him, but he holds up a hand.

"I can't trust anyone, Dana. Anyone except you." His voice softens slightly, but the intensity remains. "You're the only one I know is loyal."

He cups my face, his calloused thumb grazing my cheek. I lean into his touch, craving his strength, his protection.

"I won't let anything happen to you or Matteo," Luca vows fiercely. "You're mine, and I protect what's mine."

Possessiveness rolls off him in waves, enveloping me. I know I should bristle at his claim, but a thrill rushes through me instead.

"Stay close to me, Dana. Don't go anywhere without my permission." His grip tightens, emphasizing his command. "I need to keep you safe."

Part of me wants to argue, to assert my independence. But the vulnerability in his eyes, the desperation in his touch, silences my protests.

"I'll stay with you, Luca," I whisper, surrendering to his will. "I trust you to protect me."

Relief flashes across his face before the hard

mask slams back into place. He nods curtly, releasing me.

"Good. Go to Matteo. Don't leave his side. Now I need to find this traitor and deal with them." His tone promises violence, retribution.

Whoever the traitor is…I'm afraid even God won't be able to save them from Luca's wrath when he finds them.

———

Luca

I stalk through the estate grounds, a cold rage simmering in my veins. The traitor thinks he can hide from me, but he's a fool. I know every inch of this property, every shadow, every secret.

My men drag forward a sniveling wretch, one of the new hires for the gardens. He cowers before me, his face already bruised and bloody. They found him trying to escape, to slither away like the snake he is.

"Please, Don Romano, I didn't have a choice! They threatened my family!" he blubbers, groveling at my feet.

I crouch down, grabbing his jaw in a vise grip. "You work for me. Your loyalty is to me. And you betrayed that loyalty."

I nod to my men. They haul him to the tool shed, a soundproofed room I had installed for precisely this purpose. I roll up my sleeves methodically as he pleads and begs. I'll get the truth out of him, find out everything he told the rival family. And then I'll ensure he never betrays anyone again.

Hours later, I'm wiping blood from my hands when Marco bursts in, his face pale with alarm. "Boss, we have a situation-"

"Not now," I growl, still focused on the whimpering traitor at my feet.

"It's Dana," Marco blurts out. "They've taken her."

Ice floods my veins. I'm on my feet in an instant, the traitor forgotten. "What happened?" I demand, my voice deadly calm.

Marco swallows hard. "They came for Matteo. But Dana...she told them to take her instead. Said she was in a relationship with you, that she'd be more valuable."

A snarl rips from my throat. That foolish, brave woman. Sacrificing herself for Matteo, for *me*. Using herself as a pawn.

I'm moving before conscious thought catches up, barking orders. "Lock down the estate. No one in or out. Get me the location of every property the Rossi family owns. Alert our contacts in the police and media. I want a full press blackout."

My mind races ahead, already formulating and discarding plans. They'll expect me to come in guns blazing, but that risks Dana. No, I need to be smart about this.

My mind is racing as fear and panic unlike anything I've ever known grips me. I can't stand the thought of them hurting her. I'm going to kill every one of the motherfuckers when I get my hands on them if they've harmed one hair on her precious head.

I curse myself for putting her in danger. I should have left her alone. She'd have been better off if she'd never met me. But the thought of living without her, of never holding her soft curves against me again, never losing myself in her sweet innocence, is unbearable.

Dana is the only light in my dark, brutal world. From the moment I first saw her, her lush body and sassy smile stirring unfamiliar feelings in my jaded heart, I knew I had to have her. Had to claim her and make her *mine*.

I tried to resist, to keep my distance, knowing I would only corrupt her. Taint her goodness with the blood on my hands. But like a moth drawn to a flame, I couldn't stay away. And selfishly, I let her in, allowed her to care for Matteo, to soothe my tortured soul with her gentleness.

Now they've taken her from me. Those bastards have her, and it's my fault. I pace my study like a caged beast, a glass of scotch Marco put in my hand that I can't bring myself to drink. I know he was only trying to calm me, which says a lot about how my face must look right about now. But alcohol won't help me now. Only action will. Cold, brutal, unforgiving action.

I'll burn the city to the ground to find her if I have to. I'll call in every favor, threaten and bribe and blackmail anyone who can give me a lead. I'll torture every last member of the Rossi family until they're begging to tell me where she is.

My blood boils with a lethal cocktail of rage and terror and something even more dangerous—love. Because that's what this is, what I've been denying since she first stumbled into my life with her pretty smiles and her fierce loyalty. I love her. I fucking love her and I'll be damned if I let them take her from me.

I slam the glass down, amber liquid sloshing onto the mahogany desk. I don't have time for this, for the loathing and regret churning in my gut. I failed her, but I won't fail her again.

Dana, I'm coming, bella.

seven

. . .

Dana

THE ZIP TIES dig into my wrists as I strain against them, the plastic biting into my flesh. A metallic taste coats my tongue—fear or the aftermath of being backhanded by one of my captors, I'm not sure which.

Sweat trickles down my neck despite the dank chill in this basement room. Or warehouse. Or wherever the hell these bastards have taken me. I swallow hard, trying to quell the rising panic.

God only knows what they plan to do. Torture me? Violate me? Kill me? Bile rises in my throat at the thought.

Focus, Dana. I take a shuddering breath. *You need to be strong. For Luca. For Matteo.*

One of the men, face obscured by a black ski mask, aims a camera at me. The red recording light blinks on, taunting.

"Smile for your lover, sweetheart," he sneers. "By the time Romano gets this video, I'll have had my fill of you."

White hot rage momentarily overrides my terror. "Fuck you! Luca will kill you for this!"

"You have spirit. I'm going to enjoy breaking you." He reaches for his belt buckle and—

BAM! The door splinters open, nearly ripping off its hinges.

Like an avenging dark angel, Luca storms in, eyes wild and lethal. Before the men can even react, he seizes the one looming over me. With a roar, he smashes the man's face into his knee, crushing cartilage and bone with a sickening crunch.

Time slows as the man crumples lifelessly to the ground. More of Luca's soldiers swarm in, subduing and securing the remaining captors.

But my eyes are riveted on Luca as he rushes to me, that chiseled face etched with barely contained fury and fear.

"Dana! Cristo, what have they done to you?"

His usually steady hands shake as he cuts away my restraints.

A whimper escapes me once I'm free, my numb limbs tingling painfully. "You came," I rasp. "I knew you would."

He cradles my face with infinite tenderness, those piercing blue eyes shining with unshed tears and adoration. "Always, amore mio. Always."

Sobs wrack my body as I collapse into Luca's strong embrace, clinging to him like a lifeline. His arms encircle me protectively, one hand cradling the back of my head. I bury my face in the crook of his neck, breathing in his familiar scent of sandalwood and spice.

Safety.

Home.

"I've got you, tesoro. You're safe now," he murmurs soothingly, though I feel the tension thrumming through his powerful frame.

Pulling back slightly, Luca cups my face, his eyes roving over me searchingly. "Did they...?" He swallows hard, a muscle ticking in his clenched jaw. "Did they touch you?"

The raw anguish in his voice shatters my heart. I shake my head vehemently. "No, I'm okay. They didn't..." A shudder wracks me at the horrific memory of what almost transpired. "You stopped them in time."

Luca exhales shakily, his forehead dropping to rest against mine. "Thank God," he breathes, eyes drifting shut. "If they had...I can't even..."

"Matteo? Is he okay?" I need to confirm that he's okay.

Luca nods. "Yes, thanks to you, you stupid, brave, beautiful girl. Don't you ever do anything so dangerous again." His voice breaks with emotion.

I wind my arms around his neck and press my lips to his in a fierce, desperate kiss. He responds instantly, a low growl rumbling in his chest as he claims my mouth with searing intensity. It's a kiss of possession, of unshakable devotion. A silent vow. *You are mine and I am yours.*

"I love you," he rasps against my lips, voice raw with emotion. "I can't lose you, Dana."

"You won't," I promise breathlessly, tears clogging my throat. "I'm not going anywhere."

In wordless accord, he scoops me up, cradling me to his chest as he strides purposefully out of this hellish room, barking orders to his men. As we emerge from the warehouse into the crisp night air, I finally let myself believe it.

The nightmare is over.

I'm exactly where I belong—safe in Luca's arms.

epilogue

. . .

Two years later

Luca

I SMILE as I watch Dana chase a giggling Matteo around the sprawling garden of our countryside estate. The sun dances off her dark hair and her green eyes sparkle with joy as she scoops up my nephew in her arms, both of them laughing.

A swell of love surges through me seeing my beautiful, pregnant wife doting on the boy who has become like a son to me.

One year ago, I made the decision to step back from the dangerous world of the mafia, handing over control to my most trusted consigliere. It wasn't an easy choice, but I knew I had to put the safety and wellbeing of Dana and Matteo—and our unborn child—first. They deserved a life free from the constant threat of violence and retribution.

Dana places Matte on the swing in front of me.

"Higher, Zio Luca, higher!" Matteo squeals as I push him on the swing.

"Okay, campione, hold on tight!" I give him an extra strong push and he shrieks with glee as he soars through the air. Dana looks on, one hand resting on her round belly, a serene smile on her face.

My heart clenches at the sight. In a few short months, we'll be welcoming another child into our family. A precious girl that Dana and I created out of our incredible love for each other.

I never thought this kind of blissful domestic life would be possible for a hardened mafioso like me. But Dana changed everything. Her warmth, her strength, her unwavering faith in me.

She gave me the courage to forge a new path.

After dinner and Matteo's bedtime stories, Dana and I retreat to our bedroom, desperate to be skin to skin. I take my time undressing her, worshipping every inch of my wife's lush curves. Her pregnancy has only made her already curvy body that much fuller. Her breasts are heavy and full, tipped with dusky nipples that beg for my touch. I take one into my mouth, groaning at the first taste of sweet milk.

"Luca," she gasps, tangling her fingers in my hair.

Gently, reverently, I lay her back on our king-sized bed. She's a vision with her hair fanned out on the pillow, pink lips parted, cheeks flushed with desire. I settle between her thighs, pushing them open to reveal her wet, swollen folds.

"Ti amo, tesoro mio," I whisper before diving in to devour her sweet nectar.

My tongue explores her scorching slit, lapping, suckling, thrusting until she's writhing and keening beneath me. I slip two fingers inside her tight channel, finding that magic spot that makes her see stars. Her hands fist the sheets, and my name falls from her lips like a prayer.

"That's it, baby. Come for me," I growl against her flesh.

Her thighs clamp around my head as her orgasm crashes over in endless waves. I work her through it until she collapses boneless onto the mattress.

With a satisfied smirk, I kiss my way up her trembling body until I capture her mouth in a deep, sensual kiss. She tastes herself on my tongue and moans.

Before I can blink, Dana flips us so I'm flat on my back and she's straddling my hips. Her eyes are molten emerald as she smiles wickedly down at me. Slowly, teasingly, she shimmies down my body until she's eye level with my painfully hard cock.

"My turn," she purrs before wrapping her sweet lips around my shaft.

"Fuck, Dana!" I thrust up into the velvet heat of her mouth.

She takes me deep, swallowing around my thick length as I hit the back of her throat. My head slams back against the pillow and my hands bury themselves in her silky hair, guiding her as she bobs up and down. The sight of my innocent nanny turned wanton goddess will forever be seared in my brain.

Before I can empty down her throat, I tug her off, needing to be buried inside her. I flip her onto her hands and knees and rub the broad head of my cock through her soaked folds, coating myself in her arousal. Then with one powerful thrust, I impale her tight pussy, stretching her open.

"Yes, Luca!" she cries as I begin to pound into her.

I wrap my arm around her, splaying my hand across her pregnant belly as I continue to drill her.

My cock twitches at the knowledge that it's my child she's carrying—that *I'm* the one who fucked this baby into her perfect body.

Bending over her back, my hips maintaining their relentless rhythm, I whisper filthy, beautiful things in her ear. "You're mine, Dana. My love, my life, the mother of my children. Do you feel what you do to me? How hard you make me? I'm going to fuck this sweet cunt forever."

"Yes, yours! Only yours!" she sobs, tossing her head back.

"And these tits..." I squeeze her milk-heavy breasts and pluck at her sensitive nipples. "So full and ripe. I can't wait to suck them dry as I pump another baby into this belly."

Her pussy clenches like a vise at my dirty words and I know she's close. Reaching around, I rub tight circles over her aching clit, sending her flying over the edge with a silent scream.

Her molten walls ripple and squeeze my cock, milking me of my release. I slam into her one last time, erupting like a geyser and flooding her womb with my seed.

We collapse onto the bed, sweaty and sated. I gather my beautiful wife into my arms, softly stroking her hair and dropping kisses across her face. "Ti amo, Dana. Always and forever," I murmur.

She smiles sleepily and snuggles into my chest. "I love you too, Luca. More than anything."

As we drift off to sleep, our hands joined over her full belly, I thank the stars for giving me this incredible life. Dana and Matteo—and soon the little princess on the way—they are my heart, my home, my everything. And I will spend the rest of my days making sure they know it.

Want a free book from Emma Bray? Go to www.authoremmabray.com.

Keep reading for an excerpt from The Mobster's Obsession.

Chapter 1

Isabella

With a fluid motion, I glide across the stage, my lithe frame making each movement appear effortless. My long, dark hair is pulled back into a tight bun, adding an air of elegance to my performance. I am Isabella Hartley, a twenty-five-year-old prima ballerina who has devoted her life to dance. Each day, it consumes me, filling me with a passion I can hardly contain.

My daily routine begins at the break of dawn, when the city is still shrouded in darkness. I wake up early to prepare my body for another grueling day at the ballet company in New York City, where I practice tirelessly. I stretch my limbs, pushing them to their limits as I warm up before heading to the studio.

Once I arrive at the company, I am greeted by fellow dancers and staff members, all working toward the same goal—perfection. Our days are filled with endless rehearsals, practicing various types of dances from classical ballets like Swan Lake to more contemporary pieces that challenge our artistic abilities. As we dance, we don intricate costumes designed to evoke emotion and enhance our performances, transforming us into ethereal beings that captivate audiences.

"Morning, Isabella," one of the dancers greets

me, her eyes reflecting the spark of fierce determination that burns within us all.

"Morning," I reply, offering a small smile before diving into the day's schedule. My life revolves around these moments, the hours spent perfecting every step, every turn, every leap. It's what I live for, and I wouldn't have it any other way.

As I slip into my rehearsal attire, anticipation courses through my veins. Today, we focus on a particularly challenging piece—one that has been haunting my dreams for weeks. I yearn to master it, to conquer its complexities and make it my own.

The music begins, and I lose myself in the melody. My body moves as if possessed by the rhythm, each step executed with precision and grace. The hours fly by in a whirlwind of sweat and determination, my mind completely immersed in the world of dance.

"Isabella, remember to keep your core engaged during the arabesque," my instructor calls out, her voice firm yet encouraging. I nod, grateful for the guidance, and adjust my posture accordingly.

As the rehearsal intensifies, my body aches with each precise movement, but I refuse to let it show. Sweat trickles down my back, and the scent of rosin wafts through the air as other dancers glide across the worn wooden floor. In this cacophony of music and movement, I find solace.

"Isabella, your pirouettes are off-center," Madame Rousseau says sternly, her French accent thick and unyielding. "You must focus."

"Of course, Madame," I reply, my voice barely audible over the swell of Tchaikovsky's score. I swallow the knot in my throat and force myself to nod, acknowledging her criticism with humility. I know that she only wants me to improve, but doubt still lingers like a shadow cast upon my heart.

Steeling my nerves, I adjust the position of my feet and take a deep breath, allowing the music to envelop me once more. I can feel the eyes of my fellow company members following my every move, their silent scrutiny weighing heavily on my shoulders. I push through the discomfort, determined to prove that I am worthy of my title as prima ballerina.

"Better, Isabella," Madame Rousseau concedes, her tone softening ever so slightly. "But do not allow yourself to become complacent. There is always room for growth."

"Thank you, Madame," I murmur, my chest tightening with both gratitude and determination. I glance around the room, taking in the faces of the other dancers—some familiar, others new. Each one of us carries the same spark within us, an unwavering passion for dance that fuels our every step, our every leap into the unknown.

The sound of shoes scuffing the floor, the rustle of tulle and satin, and the hum of conversation all blend together, creating a symphony of dedication and desire. As I watch the others practice their routines, I can feel their collective energy, our shared dream of greatness, pulsing through the air like a heartbeat.

"Five minutes to break," Madame Rousseau announces, her voice cutting through the din. "Use them wisely."

I step aside, catching my breath as I wipe away the sweat from my brow. The lights in the studio cast a warm glow on the mirrors that line the walls, reflecting back the image of a young woman who refuses to cower in the face of adversity.

I stare at my reflection, my eyes dark and resolute.

I take a deep breath and grip the barre tightly, refocusing my gaze on the space before me. With each plié, each tendu, I reaffirm my commitment to this art form that has consumed my life—and my heart.

As I bend and reach for the heavens, I know

that I will never give up, no matter what challenges lie ahead. For dance is not just a passion, but a life-line—one that keeps me tethered to a world where dreams can become reality—if only we dare to push ourselves beyond the limits of what we thought possible.

"Isabella!" Madame Rousseau calls, breaking my reverie. "Back to center. It is time to continue."

"Coming, Madame," I reply, my voice steady and filled with resolve. I take one last fleeting glance at my reflection before turning away and hurrying back to rehearsal.

As the day draws to a close, I peel off my worn pointe shoes, their pink satin stained with the proof of my hard work. Exhaustion clings to me like a second skin, but I know that tomorrow, I'll be back, ready to give it my all once more.

For now, though, I allow myself a moment of reprieve, relishing the tranquility of the empty studio as I collect my belongings. Tomorrow is another day, filled with new challenges and new opportunities to grow. Another day to prove that I am worthy of being the prima ballerina who pours her heart and soul into every performance.

———

The world outside the ballet company fades away as I step through the door of my small apartment. A soft sigh escapes my lips as I sink into the worn armchair, my sanctuary after a long day of rehearsals. It's here, in this modest space that I call home, where I can finally exhale and immerse myself in the intricacies of dance, beyond the confines of the stage.

"Isabella," I whisper to myself, "you must always strive for perfection."

With the weight of my exhaustion pressing down on me like a heavy velvet curtain, I reach for the remote and turn on the television. An image of a beautifully poised dancer fills the screen, her movements fluid and powerful, as if she is one with the music. My eyes are glued to her every motion, studying her artistry, her technique, and the raw emotion etched across her face. Hours slip by as I watch video after video, each more captivating than the last.

I watch how she moves in awe and allow myself a moment of vulnerability. *I* could be that dancer one day—with enough dedication and passion.

"Passion," I repeat the word, tasting its truth on my tongue as my heart swells with a fierce determination. Dance is more than just an art form. It's a fire that burns within me, fueling my every movement and propelling me forward in this competitive world. It's what makes me feel alive, what fulfills me. When I watch these dancers, I see the possibilities.

The heights I could reach if I push myself hard enough.

———

The stage lights bathe me in a warm glow as I stand poised at the edge, my heart pounding with anticipation. The audience, a sea of shadowed faces, waits for me to bring them into my world—a world where passion and pain intertwine, where every movement tells a story.

"Isabella," whispers the ballet instructor from the wings, her eyes gleaming with expectation. "You were born for this moment. Now go and show them what you're made of."

As the first chords of Tchaikovsky's Swan Lake fill the theater, I take a deep breath and let the music guide me. It courses through my veins like liquid fire, igniting my spirit and propelling me forward. With each step, I become Odette, the tragic swan queen desperate for love and freedom.

Weaving across the stage, I execute a series of

flawless pirouettes, my lithe frame spinning like a delicate top. The audience gasps in awe, their collective breath hanging in the air like a tangible presence. In that instant, I realize that I hold their hearts in my hands, that my dance is the key to unlocking their deepest emotions.

But with great power comes great responsibility, and as I launch into a series of breathtaking leaps. my legs scissoring through the air with razor-like precision, the weight of my own expectations threatens to crush me. Will I ever be good enough? Can I truly call myself a prima ballerina if I can't silence the nagging voice inside my head that whispers, *You could do better*?

What if I fail? I think to myself as I glide effortlessly across the stage, my feet barely brushing the ground. What if all my sacrifices, all my dedication and hard work amount to nothing more than a fleeting moment of glory?

Enough! I command my inner demons, banishing them to the shadows with a fierce determination.

As the music swells to its heart-wrenching crescendo, I pour every ounce of my soul into the final pas de deux. My partner, his strong arms encircling me like a protective cocoon, lifts me high into the air, my body arching gracefully as the audience holds its breath. In this moment, suspended between heaven and earth, I know that I have conquered my fears.

"Bravo!" roars the crowd as the curtain falls, their applause thunderous in my ears. I take a deep, shuddering breath, my muscles trembling with the effort of the performance. But beneath the exhaustion lies something far more potent—a renewed sense of purpose, a burning desire to push myself to the very limits of my potential.

"I *will* be the best," I vow silently, the words etched into my very being. "No matter what it takes, I will prove to the world—and to myself— that I am worthy of the title 'prima ballerina.'"

In the darkness of the wings, the ballet instructor watches me with a knowing smile. "Well done, Isabella," she murmurs, her voice barely audible over the roar of the crowd. "You have truly outdone yourself tonight."

"Thank you," I whisper back, my eyes shining with unshed tears. "But this is only the beginning. There's so much more I have yet to achieve."

"Indeed," she replies, her gaze locked on mine. "Your journey has just begun."

———

I walk backstage, my heart pounding with the adrenaline from tonight's performance. The dancers and staff of the ballet company mill around me, their voices a chaotic symphony after the silence of the stage.

"Isabella!" A familiar voice calls out, and I turn to see my best friend, Lily, rushing toward me. Her dark curls bounce around her face as she throws her arms around me in a tight embrace. "You were absolutely incredible up there!"

"Thank you, Lily," I reply, cheeks flushing at her praise. It's hard to accept compliments when part of me still believes I have so much more to learn.

"Seriously, I'm so proud of you," she continues, eyes shining with genuine affection. "You deserve this moment."

Despite the support offered by friends like Lily, I've always had my fair share of rivals within the company. As I make my way through the crowd, I lock eyes with one of them—an icy blonde named Victoria. She smirks, her disdain evident even beneath layers of expertly applied makeup.

"Nice show, Isabella," she sneers, folding her arms across her chest. "Though I'm sure you're aware that we'll be competing for the same role next season."

"May the best dancer win," I reply coolly, not

allowing her words to pierce the armor I've built around myself. Rivalries are part of this career, but I refuse to let them define me.

As I continue to navigate the post-performance chaos, memories of my journey to becoming a prima ballerina begin to surface. My mind drifts back to the countless hours spent practicing in front of unforgiving mirrors, the ache in my muscles after every rehearsal, the sacrifices I made to get here.

"Isabella," a soft voice pulls me from my reverie. It's Madam Rousseau, our company's esteemed ballet instructor. "I must commend you on your performance tonight. You've come a long way since I first took you under my wing."

"Thank you, Madam Rousseau," I respond, ducking my head in gratitude. It was her guidance and belief in me that helped shape the dancer I am today.

"Remember when you first joined our company?" she asks, a fond smile playing on her lips. "You were so young and eager to prove yourself. And now, look at you. A true prima ballerina."

Her words take me back to those early days. The excitement mixed with fear as I stepped into this world of fierce competition and unrelenting expectations. I had been determined to prove myself, to show that I belonged among these exceptional artists. And through sheer grit and determination, I managed to do just that.

"None of it would have been possible without your guidance, Madame," I tell her, my voice thick with emotion. "You believed in me when no one else did, and for that, I am eternally grateful."

"Believe in yourself, Isabella," she advises, her eyes locking onto mine. "That is the key to unlocking your full potential."

The truth in her words resonates within me, and I nod, vowing to never lose faith in my abilities, no matter what challenges lie ahead.

―――――

My passion for dance has always been a double-edged sword, slicing through my personal life with the precision of a ballet dancer's pointed toe. As I leave the ballet company building, I can't help but feel a pang of guilt for what my dedication to the art has cost me.

"Isabella, wait up!" a familiar voice calls out, and I turn to see Michael, a long-time friend and confidant who has always been there for me. He jogs to catch up, a warm smile on his face.

"Hey, Michael," I greet him, trying to ignore the

nagging thoughts of how my devotion to the ballet company has left little room for anything else in my life.

"Are you free tonight? We could grab dinner and catch up," he suggests, hope glinting in his eyes. But I hesitate, knowing that I've canceled on him too many times before. The thought of another evening spent going over dance theory or watching videos of other dancers beckons me like an irresistible siren's song.

"Michael, I..." I trail off, struggling to find the right words. "You know how much dance means to me. It's just...it consumes me, every waking moment."

He sighs, disappointment etched across his face as he runs a hand through his hair. "I get it, Isabella. I really do. It's just hard sometimes, feeling like I'm competing with your passion for dance."

"I'm sorry," I whisper, my heart heavy with guilt. My inability to maintain a romantic relationship weighs on me, but the magnetic pull of the ballet world is impossible to resist.

"Hey, don't be," he smiles gently, placing a hand on my shoulder. "I'll always be here for you, Bella. Just...try to remember there's more to life than the stage, okay?"

"Thank you, Michael," I breathe, grateful for his

understanding. But even as we part ways, my thoughts are already wandering back to the ballet company and the life I've chosen.

That night, as I stretch my limbs in preparation for another day of rehearsals, I receive a call from Madame Rousseau. Her tone is hushed, full of anticipation. "Isabella, there's something I need to share with you."

"Of course, Madame," I respond, my curiosity piqued.

"There are rumors we're getting a new owner," she reveals, her voice thick with excitement. "You must make a good impression, Isabella. This could be the opportunity of a lifetime."

As I hang up the phone, my pulse races, adrenaline coursing through my veins. This could be my chance to reach new heights, to prove myself as a dancer beyond the walls of the ballet company. I feel a pang as I think of the personal sacrifices I've made, though, and the potential relationships I've left behind.

But as I glance at my reflection in the mirror, my eyes dark and determined, I know that I have no choice. Dance is my life, my very essence, and I will do whatever it takes to grasp the opportunities that come my way—even if it means losing myself in the process.

. . .

Chapter 2

Vincenzo

The rain falls like a thousand dark teardrops from the sky, soaking me as I stand outside my luxurious penthouse overlooking the city that bows to my will. My name is Vincenzo De Luca, and I rule this concrete jungle with an iron grip. At forty-five years old, I've earned my reputation as a notorious mob boss, feared by many and respected by all who know of me.

As I light my Cuban cigar, its smoke swirling around me like a sinister haze, I think about my vast network of criminal activities that stretch across every corner of the city. From the dark alleyways where drugs change hands to the high-stakes poker games in exclusive clubs, my influence is felt everywhere. The docks, controlled by my loyal soldiers, handle shipments of illegal weapons and smuggled goods. The corrupt politicians in their ivory towers bend to my whims, ensuring that law enforcement turns a blind eye to my dealings. Even the judges tremble at the sound of my name, knowing full well that my reach extends into the very heart of the justice system.

I take a long drag of my cigar and exhale slowly, savoring the taste of power on my lips. It's a bitter pleasure, one that has cost me dearly over the years. But there's no denying that it's also intoxicating, like a fine wine aged in blood and betrayal.

My control over this city is absolute, but even I have my weaknesses. There are times when I question the choices I've made, the lives I've destroyed to get where I am today. But in the end, it's the game that keeps me going—the thrill of outmaneuvering my enemies and asserting my dominance over those who would dare challenge me.

And yet, as I stand here in the pouring rain, feeling the weight of my empire bearing down on me, I can't help but wonder if there's more to life than this. Is there something beyond the darkness that consumes me, a light waiting to break through the shadows of my soul?

The rain continues to fall, washing away the sins of the city below. But for me, Vincenzo De Luca, king of the underworld, the stains of my past can never truly be cleansed.

———

I step into my private gallery, a sanctuary of beauty in a world full of darkness. The walls are adorned with priceless paintings from the Renaissance, each one a testament to the genius of mankind. I've always had a fondness for art and culture—they represent a side of humanity that transcends our baser instincts, allowing us to create something truly eternal.

"Vincenzo!" my consigliere, Marco, calls out as he enters the gallery, interrupting my reverie. "We have a problem."

"What is it?" I ask, my eyes scanning the master-pieces before me, seeking solace in their vibrant colors and timeless grace.

"Antonio's shipment was intercepted by the police," he replies, his voice tense. "They confiscated everything—weapons, drugs, you name it."

"Antonio," I snarl, the anger bubbling within me like molten lava. "That imbecile's incompetence will cost us dearly."

"Indeed," agrees Marco. "But we can still salvage this situation if we act quickly."

"Bring Antonio to me," I command, feeling the familiar surge of adrenaline as I prepare to assert my authority once more. "And gather the rest of the crew. It's time to remind them who's in charge here."

As I wait for Antonio to be brought before me, I pace the gallery, surrounded by the serene visages of saints and martyrs. Their placid expressions seem at odds with the brutal reality of my life, but somehow, their presence calms me. In this hallowed space, I can almost forget the blood on my hands, the screams that echo through my dreams.

"Please, Vincenzo," Antonio pleads, his eyes wide with fear as he's dragged into the room. "It wasn't my fault! The cops were tipped off. There was nothing I could do!"

"Silence!" I roar, my voice like a thunderclap in the quiet gallery. "You have failed me for the last time, Antonio. Do you understand what that means?"

"Please," he whispers, tears streaming down his face. "I'll do anything to make it right."

"Anything?" I ask, my eyes narrowing as I consider his fate. "Very well. You will serve as an example to the others—a reminder of the consequences of failure."

"Vincenzo... no," he whimpers, but his pleas fall on deaf ears.

"Take him away," I order, my heart heavy with the weight of my decision. Even after all these years, the taste of betrayal still lingers, bitter and cold on my tongue. But as I gaze upon the masterpieces before me, I find solace in their beauty once more. For in this world of darkness, even the most ruthless of men can find refuge in the light of art and culture.

———

My fingers trace the delicate edges of a porcelain figurine, its intricate details a testament to the artist's skill. Surrounded by countless masterpieces, I find myself momentarily lost in their beauty, as if my world of darkness has been briefly shattered by the light of the divine. But even here, in the sanctuary of my private collection, there is no escaping the shadows that cling to me like a heavy cloak.

"Vincenzo?" A hesitant voice interrupts my reverie.

"Speak," I command, my tone as sharp as a blade, though my eyes never leave the fragile statuette before me.

"The girl...the prima ballerina, Isabella, has been asking about you, sir," says Marco, my most trusted lieutenant.

At the mention of her name, my heart tightens, and I can feel the icy grip of vulnerability clawing at my chest. Isabella, my dark obsession, my forbidden desire—the one chink in the armor I have so carefully crafted over the years.

"I'll take care of it," I reply, the words tasting like ash on my tongue.

"Very well, Vincenzo," Marco bows and retreats from the room, leaving me alone with my thoughts.

I force myself to shake off the unsettling feeling that her concern has stirred within me. I am Vincenzo De Luca, feared and respected mob boss, ruler of this city's underworld. My cold blue eyes have witnessed unspeakable acts, my hands stained with the blood of those who dared defy me. The slicked-back dark hair peppered with gray that crowns my head serves as a constant reminder of the battles I've fought, both visible and invisible. And yet, despite my power and influence, it is the innocence of Isabella that has the power to bring me to my knees.

As I pace through my gallery, the vivid paintings and ancient sculptures seem to mock me, their beauty a stark contrast to the darkness that consumes my soul. I can sense the restless energy coursing through my veins, the need for control burning like an unquenchable fire within me.

"Isabella," I whisper her name, as if it were a prayer, and my chest tightens once more.

"Vincenzo!" Marco's voice echoes through the

gallery, panic lacing his words. "You must come quickly! We have a problem."

"Damn it!" I curse under my breath, the sudden intrusion an unwelcome reminder of the demands of my life. My heart hammers in my chest, a mixture of anger and anxiety fueling my every step as I stride toward the door.

My world is a twisted web of darkness and deceit, a place where trust is a currency few can afford. As I walk through the familiar shadows of my empire, I can't help but reflect on how I came to find myself here—at the helm of an unstoppable force that has consumed everything in its path.

I was just a boy when I entered this life, seeking refuge from the cruelty of my father's fists. The streets became my home, and I learned quickly that only the strong survive. It was there amongst the filth and desperation that I met Don Antonio, a man who saw potential in my rage and ruthlessness. He took me under his wing, and together we forged a new path.

One paved with blood and betrayal.

Over time, our enemies fell before us, their empires crumbling beneath the weight of our ambition. We were feared and respected, our names whispered in hushed tones throughout the city. And yet, despite our victories, there was always a gnawing emptiness within me—a hunger that could not be sated by power alone.

"Vincenzo," Don Antonio once said to me, his eyes dark and solemn, "a man must find balance in his life, lest he be consumed by the very darkness he seeks to control."

And so, I began my journey into the world of art and culture, seeking solace in the beauty of creation. My collection grew over the years, each piece a testament to the human spirit's ability to rise above despair. In this sanctuary, I found peace —a fleeting moment of respite amidst the chaos of my existence.

As I deal with the "problem"—which is indeed a problem but is hardly worth the panic Marco infused into the situation— my thoughts return to Isabella, the innocent beauty who has captured my obsession. In her eyes, I see a reflection of the purity I crave yet can never attain. It is both a torment and a comfort, this strange yearning for redemption.

I remember the first time I saw her. Her lithe little form dancing across the stage.

A rare beauty.

It was more than her figure, though. More than that beautiful brown hair that flowed all the way down to her waist and swayed behind her as she floated across the stage soft as a feather.

There was something so innocent yet so fierce in her crystalline blue eyes.

I had never been one to believe in love at first sight, but the moment I laid eyes on her, I knew she was the missing piece to my fragmented soul. With each passing day, my obsession with her grew stronger, my desire to possess her consuming every waking thought.

And yet, despite my best efforts, she remained elusive, slipping through my grasp like sand through my fingers. It was as though the universe was taunting me, offering up a prize that could never be mine.

But I refuse to accept defeat. I *will* have her. I will make her mine, no matter the cost.

As I sit in my dark and opulent study, surrounded by the trappings of my power and wealth, I think of her. My Isabella. I imagine her slender frame pressed against mine, her soft lips parting beneath my touch. The thought alone is enough to make my blood boil, my body aching with need.

And so, I make a decision. A decision that will change the course of our futures forever.

I will have her, even if I must tear down the world to do so.

———

The rain lashes against the floor-to-ceiling windows as I stand in my opulent study, the tempest outside mirroring my own inner turmoil. My hand absently caresses the silk-covered spine of a worn, ancient book on the shelf, as if seeking solace in its time-worn familiarity. The scent of leather and old parchment fills my nostrils, momentarily drawing me away from my darker thoughts.

"Vincenzo," a gravelly voice calls out, pulling me back to the present. It's Marco, my most trusted lieutenant, his face etched with concern. "You've been locked away in here for hours. Is everything alright? The men are getting restless."

"Let them be restless," I snap, irritated at the intrusion. "They're not the ones who have to make the decisions around here." I pause, staring out at the stormy night as I collect my thoughts. "It's Isabella, Marco. She's...different. I feel this...vulnerability whenever I'm near her. It gnaws at me, eats away at the very core of my being."

"Love can do that to a man, boss," he says cautiously, shifting uncomfortably in his expensive suit. "But you've gotta keep your head straight. We've got business to handle, and our enemies won't wait for you to sort out your feelings."

"Feelings?" I scoff, turning to face him. "This isn't about feelings, Marco. It's about power, control, and the delicate balance that holds everything together. That girl has the potential to shatter it all, and I'm not sure I'm prepared to stop her."

"Then maybe you should let her in," he suggests, meeting my icy gaze with his own steely resolve. "Show her who you really are, the man behind the empire. Maybe she'll surprise you."

"Or maybe she'll run screaming into the night," I counter, clenching my fists in frustration. "I can't risk it, Marco. I've spent my entire life building this empire, and I refuse to let it crumble because of some misguided infatuation."

"Then you've got a choice to make, boss," he says bluntly, his loyalty never wavering. "You can either keep hiding behind your walls, or you can face whatever vulnerability she stirs up and come out stronger for it. The decision is yours."

His words resonate within me as I look back out at the storm, the raindrops streaking down the glass like tears on a lover's face. Isabella has awakened something inside me, something I thought had died long ago under the weight of blood and betrayal.

She's brought light into my world of darkness, and I find myself torn between the desire to protect her innocence and the need to possess her completely.

"Thank you, Marco," I say quietly, my voice barely audible above the howling wind. "You've given me much to consider."

"Whatever you decide, boss," he replies, his loyalty unwavering. "I'm with you all the way."

As he leaves the room, I remain standing by the window, lost in thought. My heart wars with my mind, each vying for control over my actions. In the end, only one thing is certain: Isabella has changed me irrevocably, and there's no turning back now.

———

The rain has finally stopped, leaving behind the scent of wet earth and damp asphalt. I step out onto my balcony overlooking the city, inhaling deeply, feeling the cool breeze brush against my face, carrying with it the distant sound of traffic and laughter from the streets below. My world is alive with sensation, each one a reminder that life goes on despite the storm raging inside my heart.

"Boss?" Marco's voice intrudes upon my reverie, and I turn to find him standing in the doorway, his concern evident in the furrow of his brow. "You've been out here for hours. You should come inside and get some rest."

"I'm fine," I reply tersely, my gaze drifting back to the cityscape spread out before me like a canvas waiting to be painted with passion and violence. The glow of the moon casts eerie shadows across the skyline, illuminating the darker corners where secrets hide and desires fester. It's far too late for rest now.

"Your fascination with art and culture won't save you from what's coming, boss," Marco warns, his voice barely above a whisper. "You can't keep ignoring the threats to your empire."

"Neither can I ignore the call of my heart," I admit, clenching my fists at my sides as I struggle to reconcile these conflicting passions—the ruthless mob boss who rules with an iron fist, and the man whose soul yearns for the beauty and grace of Isabella's touch.

"Is she worth it?" he asks, his words echoing my own thoughts.

"Only time will tell," I respond, my voice heavy with doubt and longing. "But I can't deny her any longer, no matter the cost."

"Then let's hope you're prepared to pay the

price," Marco says grimly, turning to leave me alone with my thoughts once more.

As I stand there, the wind picking up once more and stirring the night air, I can't help but feel a sense of foreboding, as if something dark and dangerous is waiting just around the corner. But the pull toward Isabella is too strong to resist, her innocence a beacon in the cold, unforgiving world I inhabit.

"Isabella," I murmur into the wind, my heart aching with the weight of decisions made and roads taken. "I will protect you from the darkness that threatens to consume us both."

With each gust, the promise lingers on the breeze, intertwining with the distant sounds of the city below—a symphony of desire and danger, of love and war. The storm inside me rages on, but for now, I am at peace with the knowledge that my path has been chosen, and only fate knows what lies ahead.

As I step back inside and close the door behind me, sealing off the balcony from the increasingly turbulent night, I can't help but wonder if I've already set in motion events that will change our lives forever. The anticipation coils within me, a serpent ready to strike. In the end, only one thing is certain: the darkness is coming, and I must be prepared to face it head-on, no matter the cost.